1835

1910

PB's Comet

PB's Comet

Written by Marnie Parsons

Illustrated by Veselina Tomova

Down, down drove the truck, with one goat and some sheep,

down the twisty old road to Toads Cove's harbour deep.

Over the water, in a creaky wee boat,

went the lambs and the sheep and the grumpy old goat.

Off to Fox Island, with its water so sweet

and its salty green grass, for a few months' retreat.

But while the rest lingered on the steep steep incline,
watched the whales and the birds, and the tourists sometimes—
who watched them right back, if the truth were to be known—
one little lamb would be off on her own.

PB was, you see, a lamb of a more serious sort.
Oh, she'd nibble the grass and would sometimes cavort
on the rocks by the sea with the sheep and the goat,
but her interests reached further than the whales and tour boats
that sailed past the island where the sheep summered each year,
relaxing and grazing, with nothing to fear,
and the occasional visit, at an especially low tide,
from neighbours who lived on the Cribbies side.

More often than not the other sheep found

PB, with a book, hove off on the ground,

and when they'd insist that she leave off and come play,

she'd point a hoof skyward, and solemnly say

Edmond
Halley

that Toads Cove had once welcomed a man who watched stars,

who measured the distances between near and far,

and who knew when a comet would shoot through the sky,

and if he could, well then, PB said, "So can I!"

So she studied star maps and she stayed up all night
with a special spy glass, and she spied 'til the light
of day peeked over the water and finally crested—
and then, quite exhausted, she lay down and rested.

But when the sun settled low and the moon climbed up high,
she'd speculate carefully just when, by and by,
another spectacular star might shoot high
dragging its tail across the night sky.

PB made calculations, predictions, and claims,
quite certain this knowledge would lead to her fame;
and charted and graphed and grappled with math—
until she was sure she had found the path
that one day quite soon a new comet would follow:

But all of her theories were some lot to swallow
for her comrades and friends, and especially the goat,
who was inclined to be grumpy and rather remote.

'A stick in the mud,' the others called him most days;
he was undoubtedly set in his goat-y old ways.
And an upstart young lamb with her head full of stars
was too much for this old goat to stomach, by far.

So he'd hide PB's spyglass and munch on her maps
and jumble her numbers while poor PB napped.
But no matter the ills of the old goat's devising,
PB maintained an extremely surprising
insistence that soon her comet would come,
and with every assurance that goat seemed more glum.

The Evening Sky Map

Still he'd chew and he'd grumble and he'd ruminate
on a way to unravel PB's plans for the date
when the comet's arrival would brighten the heavens.

But with each passing day he was at sixes and sevens,
seeing no possible way to arrange PB's comeuppance
and the day fast approaching; 'til a casual glance
up at the sky one crisp and clear night
made him pause to consider a beautiful sight…

He was an old goat, I believe I have said,
and old goats are often the first ones to bed.
For the past many years he'd nod off by sunset,
and this silly old goat had come to forget

the sight of the night sky, and the wonder it brings
of the largeness and the beauty and the smallness of things.

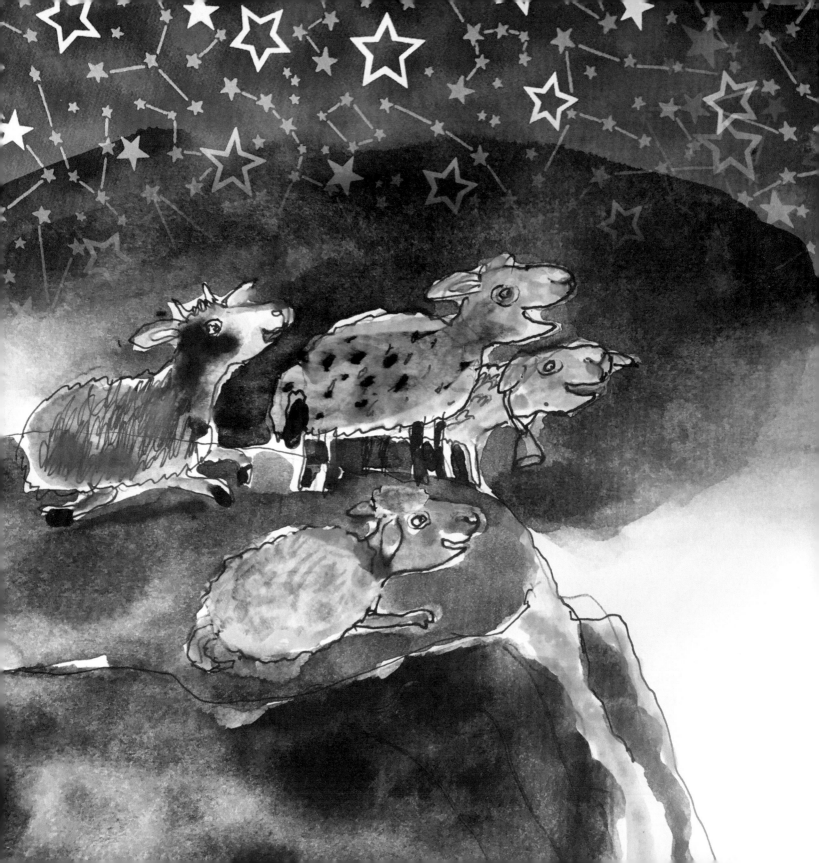

So caught up in his plotting he missed his bedtime—
and then rapt by this vision he started to climb
up the steep steep incline to the island's high spot
to precisely the place where young PB sot,
awaiting her comet, with her charts and her graphs,
while at the edge of the cliff the other sheep laughed.

PB smiled a welcome, the goat settled in,

and looked up at the stars with a hesitant grin.

It wasn't much later when the old goat gave a nod,

raised a hoof skyward, and sighed, truly awed.

It sat low in the sky, but clearly was there,

A light with a bright and a brilliant tail, where

The other stars seemed all distant and dim—

"What's that constellation," he asked, on a whim.

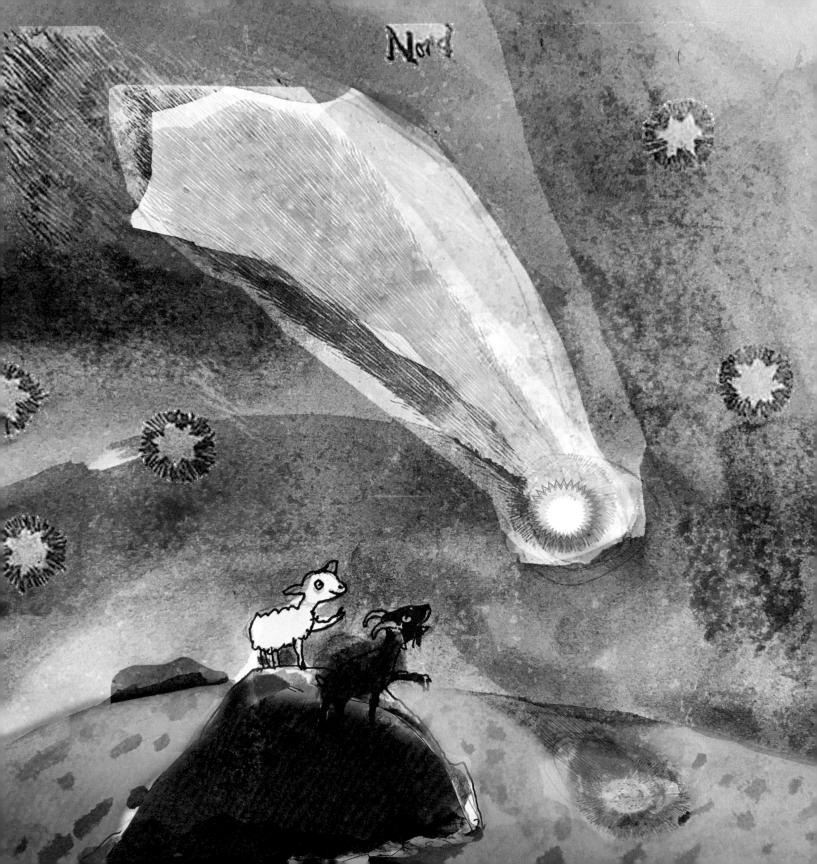

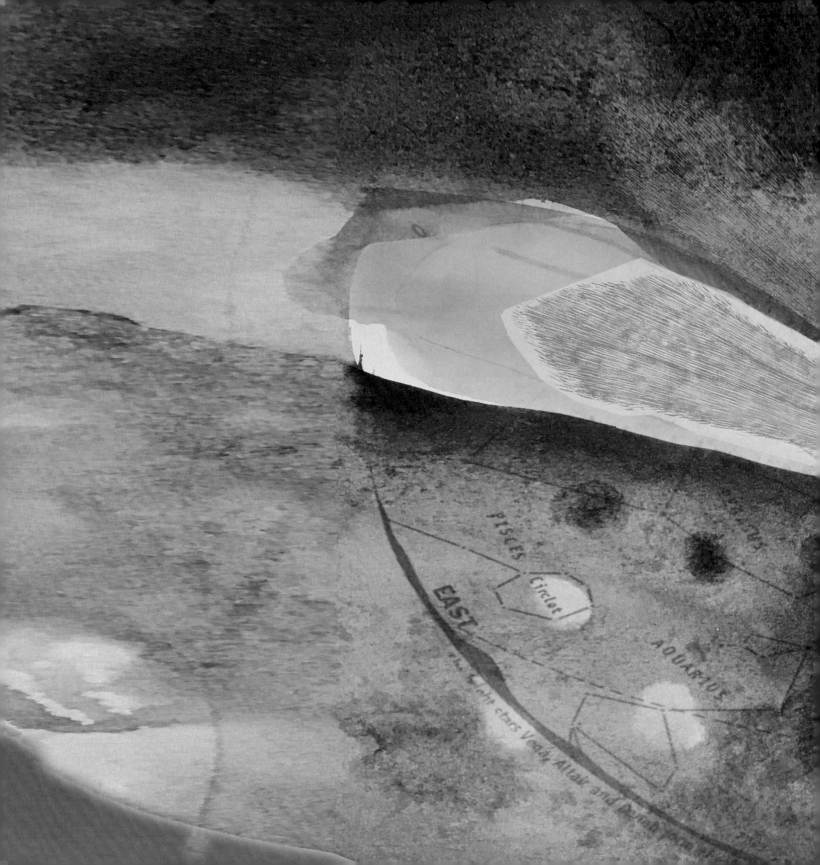

After checking her sky map, PB cleared her throat:

"Seems our comet's been swallowed by the 'Sea Goat.'"

The other sheep all gave off laughing and teasing,
but they didn't find stargazing terribly pleasing.
They were quite content just to nibble and graze,
continuing on in their same sheep-ish ways.
And while they admitted PB had been right,
they rarely joined her and the goat of a night
to watch the skies darken and the stars all come out.

But as to that goat, well, he no longer had doubts—

So now every evening before heading for bed,
he studies the stars, and recalls how PB said,
she could trace a comet through the summer night sky,
and with a crooked wee grin, the goat says, "So can I!"

NOTES

The man whose story inspired PB to search the skies was English astronomer
Edmond Halley, who briefly visited Toads Cove, an outport on Newfoundland's
Avalon Peninsula, in August of 1700 while on a journey of scientific discovery.
Halley made many important contributions to scientific knowledge,
but he is most famous for accurately predicting the return of the comet
that bears his name. My maternal grandmother recalled seeing Halley's comet,
as a young girl, in the early spring of 1910.

It was also in 1910 that Toads Cove was renamed Tors Cove. Every year local
farmers take their sheep out to two of the islands just off the coast—Fox Island
and Ship Island—to graze for the summer. The Cribbies is the local name
for land just opposite Fox Island.

"The Sea Goat" is another name for the constellation Capricornus, which
can be seen in the northern sky in late summer.

PB is named for another island near Tors Cove, but that's another story.
                    ~ Marnie Parsons

ACKNOWLEDGEMENTS

Thanks to Jane Severs, who inadvertently gave PB her name.

The tourist cow is for Darka Erdelji, Andy Jones, and Mary-Lynn Bernard, with love.

Boundless thanks to Sandy Newton, for kind suggestions that pushed this story further; to Tara Bryan, Rachel Dragland, and Sheree Fitch, for encouragement and enthusiasm; to Don McKay, for careful reading and for saying "it's about time"; and to Veselina Tomova, for bringing *PB's Comet* to life, and for making the whole Goat adventure so much fun.

~ M.P.

Big thanks to Marnie Parsons for quietly and steadfastly advancing on her quest to publish books of quality, and giving me the pleasure to illustrate and design stories close to my heart. And to all my friends on the Southern Shore who made me fall in love with its fog, flocks, and rocks.

~ V.T.

This book was designed by Veselina Tomova
of Vis-à-vis Graphics, St. John's, Newfoundland and Labrador,
and printed by Friesens in Canada.

978-1-927917-12-1

Running the Goat is grateful to Newfoundland and Labrador's Department of Tourism,
Culture, Industry and Innovation for support of its publishing activities
through the province's Publishers Assistance Program.

Newfoundland
Labrador

Running the Goat
Books & Broadsides Inc.
54 Cove Road / General Delivery
Tors Cove, Newfoundland and Labrador A0A 4A0
www.runningthegoat.com